IGOR'S LAB OF FEAR

MAZE MONSTER

by Michael Dahl   illustrated by Andy Catling

Raintree is an imprint of Capstone Global Library Limited, a company
incorporated in England and Wales having its registered office at
264 Banbury Road, Oxford, OX2 7DY – Registered company number:
6695582

www.raintree.co.uk
myorders@raintree.co.uk

ISBN 978-1-4747-2534-7 (paperback)
20 19 18 17 16
10 9 8 7 6 5 4 3 2 1

British Library Cataloguing in Publication Data
A full catalogue record for this book is available from the British
Library.

COVER ILLUSTRATOR: Igor Šinkovek
DESIGNER: Kristi Carlson
EDITORS: Sean Tulien and Abby Colich

Printed in China.

CONTENTS

Who goes there?!

Go away! You'll set off one of my traps.

Watch your step. Or you'll end up in a pit of rats!

Oh, I'm sorry. It's just you
again.

<u>Wonderful!</u> Come in, come in.

What? A pit filled with rats?
Oh, I was only joking.

I'd never put poor little rats in a pit. He-he.

Speaking of rats, do you see that wedge of cheese?

There's an **INTERESTING** story behind it...

CHAPTER ONE:
BREAK-IN

Ned and Victor were near a parking lot.

They hid behind some bushes.

They watched a nearby building. Men and women left, got into their cars, and drove away.

Soon, the last car left the car park.

The two boys left their hiding place.

They ran to the side of the building.

"There!" said Ned.

He pointed up at a window.

"Let's try it!" Victor said.

Victor gave Ned a leg-up.

Ned gripped the windowsill. He pulled on the glass.

The window opened easily. Its hinges were smooth and quiet.

"Those scientists never lock them," said Ned.

Both boys **QUICKLY** climbed inside.

CHAPTER TWO:
THE STRANGE ROOM

"What is all this stuff?" asked Victor.

Inside, the boys looked around. WEIRD glass containers sat on tables.

Plastic tubes ran around the entire room.

Several machines had colourful wires. Metal rods stuck out from them.

The walls were covered with computer screens.

"What do they do with all this stuff?" Victor asked.

"Experiments," said Ned. "You know, like in science lessons."

Victor leaned in to examine a container. A weird **BLOB** floated inside. It looked like a hairless rat.

"Um," Victor said. "What kind of experiments?"

The blobby thing in the jar flinched. "Ah!" Victor cried, jumping back. His arm bumped the jar. It fell to the floor.

CRASH!

"Be careful!" Ned hissed. "The guards will hear us!"

Some of the goo had splashed on Victor's hands. He wiped them on his shirt. "Yuck," he said. "It smells like rotten cheese."

The boys heard a door slam somewhere in the building.

"Oh, great," whispered Ned. "One of the guards heard you."

"What do we do now?" said Victor.

CHAPTER THREE:
ESCAPE

"Quick!" said Ned. "Do you have a penny?"

Victor dug into his pockets. Finally, he pulled out a coin.

"Here," he said. He dropped the penny into Ned's palm. "But why do you want..."

"Shh," said Ned. "Just keep quiet and follow me."

The boys crept into the hall.

They heard another door slam.
They **RAN** in the opposite direction.

They tried to open each door
along the hall. But all of them were
locked.

Except for one. A door with a sign on it.

KEEP OUT!
SPECIAL SCIENCE
TEAM ONLY

"Maybe the guard won't follow us in there," said Ned.

Victor nodded. He pushed the door open.

The boys **RUSHED** inside.

CHAPTER FOUR:
IT'S A TRAP!

They heard the guard walk past the door.

Ned held the penny in his fist.

A moment later, he opened the door.

He threw the penny down the hall.

It hit a far wall. **CLINK!**

They heard the guard rushing back the way he'd come. Ned quietly closed the door.

"Why'd you do that?" whispered Victor.

"To distract him," said Ned. "If he keeps looking over there, he won't find us."

Victor sniffed. "Hey," he said. "What's that smell? It's making me hungry."

"Yeah, what is that?" asked Ned. "Pizza?"

MMMMMMMMMMMMMMMMMMMM

The boys walked farther into the room.

They found another door. It was dark and made of metal.

"The smell's coming from in there," said Victor.

They opened the metal door and entered.

As it closed behind them, they heard a loud **CLICK!**

"It locked behind us," said Victor. "We're trapped!"

CHAPTER FIVE:
MAZE RUNNERS

The locked door was made of steel.

"We can't break that door down," Victor said.

Ned **GULPED**. "Not a problem," he said. "We'll just find another way out."

As they looked around, they realised they were not in a room. Instead, it was a long, **DARK** hallway.

The hall was lined with lots of open doors.

"That's weird," said Victor. "That smell is gone."

Both boys stopped and sniffed.

"I smell something else," said Ned. "And it STINKS!"

"Let's get going," said Victor. "We've got to get out of here."

The boys chose the first door on the left.

They entered, and found themselves in another hall. Even more open doors lined the walls.

The boys went in another door. The same kind of hall awaited them.

They entered door after door. Each one led to more halls with more doors.

Soon, they hit a dead end.

They had to go back and find another route.

After about an hour of walking, Victor gagged.

"The smell!" he shouted. He pointed at the floor.

A pile of round, smelly blobs lay there.

Each blob was the size of a football.

"Ew," said Ned. "That smells like dog poo."

"I think that's exactly what it is," said Victor.

"No dog is big enough to make those," said Ned.

ROAR!

The boys looked up. Down at the other end of the hall, two red dots of light appeared.

The red dots grew larger and larger.

"What is that?!" screamed Ned.

A white, red-eyed rat bared its teeth. A wheel of cheese fell from its jaws.

Its beady eyes examined the boys. Drool dripped from its incisors.

They turned and ran.

Ned and Victor should never have snuck into the lab.

Sure, they were just curious. But you know what they say about curiosity … he-he.

Luckily, I heard the boys survived.
They are helping the scientists with
some brand new experiments.

The scientists are learning a lot
from their new *lab brats!*

He-he. Heh Heh Heh Heh

PROFESSOR IGOR'S LAB NOTES

Ever wonder what happens in a laboratory? Don't break into one like Ned and Victor did to find out. Let me tell you. After all, I'm an expert in the lab...

Most laboratories are used for research or for developing new products. Doctors may work in a laboratory to identify diseases or make new medicines. Engineers may work in a lab, building new robots or rockets. Some students work in labs to further their studies.

The equipment inside of a laboratory depends on what research the scientists inside are doing. Supplies can range from Petri dishes and test tubes to huge, complex computers.

The scientists inside labs take many safety precautions. They may wear gloves, goggles, or even rubber suits to protect themselves. Some labs may contain secret information. Extreme security measures are often in place. Unlocked doors and windows at night are very unlikely. Seems like the scientists who work in the lab Ned and Victor broke into weren't being very careful. Maybe they were even hoping two young boys would try to break in. He-he...

GLOSSARY

BARE to lack a cover

BEADY small, round, and shiny, resembling beads

CURIOUS eager to explore and learn about new things

DISTRACT to draw attention away from something

FLINCH to quickly and suddenly jerk or move away

GAG to vomit or feel like vomiting

INCISOR front tooth used for cutting

PIT a hole in the ground

ROUTE a road or path followed to get somewhere

STEEL a hard, strong metal

WEDGE a piece of food that is narrow at one end and thick at the other

DISCUSSION QUESTIONS

1. After Ned and Victor distracted the guard, they smelled something. What do you think that smell was? Where was it coming from?

2. What do you think Professor Igor means at the end of the story when he says that Ned and Victor were just curious? Use the definition of curious in the Glossary to help you answer the question.

3. Do you think Ned and Victor got what they deserved for breaking into the lab? Explain why or why not.

WRITING PROMPTS

1. Write a paragraph about a time you felt like you were caught in a maze or trapped somewhere. Talk about the feelings you had during this time.

2. How do you think the rat in the laboratory got so large? Write a short story about what happened to the rat in the lab.

3. What happens next in the story? You decide! Write another chapter about what happens next to Ned and Victor in the lab. Use the picture on page 35 to spark your imagination.

AUTHOR BIOGRAPHY

Michael Dahl, the author of the Library of Doom, Dragonblood, and Troll Hunters series, has a long list of things he's afraid of: dark rooms, small rooms, damp rooms (all of which describe his writing area), storms, rabid squirrels, wet paper, raisins, flying in planes (especially taking off, cruising, and landing), and creepy dolls. He hopes that by writing about fear he will eventually be able to overcome his own. So far it isn't working. But he is afraid to stop, so he continues to write. He lives in a haunted house in Minneapolis, Minnesota.

ILLUSTRATOR BIOGRAPHY

Andy Catling is a professional scribbler and splurger of pictures who has illustrated for publishers around the world. Andy works in traditional mediums and digital wot-nots using a rigorous mangle-like process. First he draws a picture. Then he rubs it out and draws it again. He colours using watercolour, pencils, and ink, sniffs it, screws it up, and starts over. The digital work process is much the same but without the sniffing. (All digital artwork smells of screen wipe.) Andy lives in the United Kingdom. He thinks he is a pirate.